A Quick Buzz

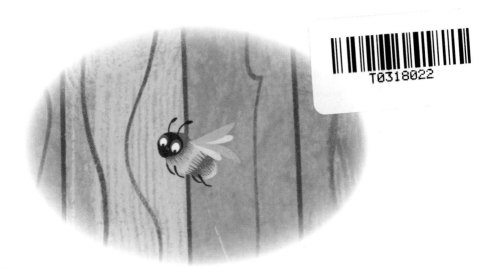

Written by Caroline Green
Illustrated by Thaís Mesquita

Collins

a thin dog

long legs

a thin dog

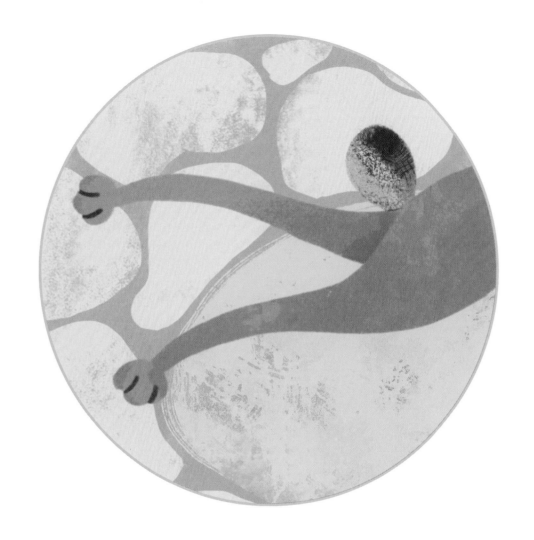

long legs

a shut shed

a pink jug

a shut shed

a pink jug

a wet cat

a quick buzz

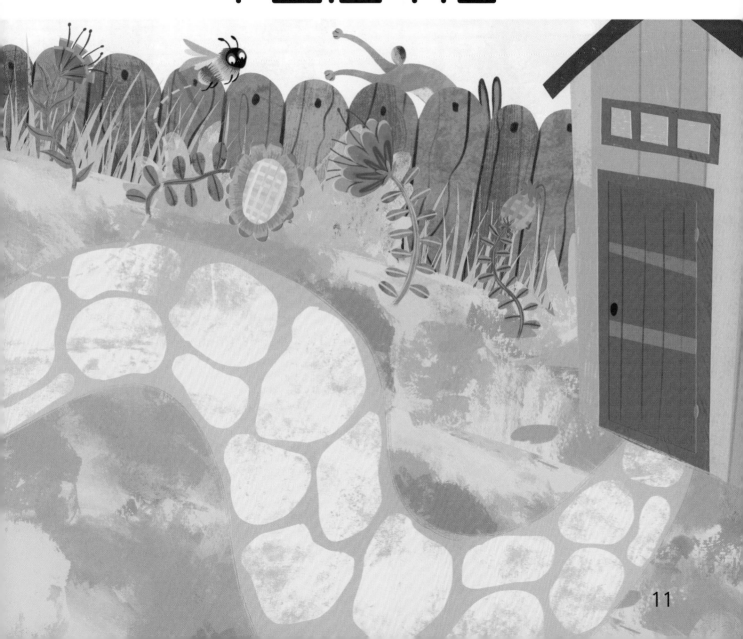

a wet cat

a quick buzz

/j/

14

/nk/

 Review: After reading

Use your assessment from hearing the children read to choose any GPCs or words that need additional practice.

Read 1: Decoding
- Use grapheme cards to make any words you need to practise. Model reading those words, using teacher-led blending.
- Look at the "I spy sounds" pages (14–15) together. Ask the children to point out as many things as they can in the picture that begin with the /j/ sound or end with the /nk/ sound. (*jug, juice, jewel, jellybeans, jelly, jar, jam, jellyfish, jeans, jigsaw; drink, tank, pink, ink*)
- Ask the children to follow as you read the whole book, demonstrating fluency and prosody.

Read 2: Vocabulary
- Look back through the book and discuss the pictures. Encourage the children to talk about details that stand out for them. Use a dialogic talk model to expand on their ideas and recast them in full sentences as naturally as possible.
- Work together to expand vocabulary by naming objects in the pictures that children do not know.
- Read page 2 and ask: What else can you see in the picture that is thin? (e.g. *flower stem, flower petals, blades of grass, path, window, hare's ears*)

Read 3: Comprehension
- Reread pages 2 and 3. Talk about the animals and what they are doing. Ask the children: Have you seen animals like these chasing each other outside, on television or in a book? Have you played a game of chase? What happened?
- Reread pages 10 and 11. Talk about what has happened. Prompt with questions, such as: Why is the cat wet? (e.g. *the jug fell over*) What made a quick buzz? (*a bee*) Why is the hare jumping over the fence? (e.g. *to get away from the bee*)